A Heartbeat Away

The Doctor's Dilemma Collection, Volume 1

Dr. Nilesh Panchal

Published by DrMedHealth, 2024.

This is a work of fiction. Similarities to real people, places, or events are entirely coincidental.

A HEARTBEAT AWAY

First edition. October 21, 2024.

Copyright © 2024 Dr. Nilesh Panchal.

ISBN: 979-8227576088

Written by Dr. Nilesh Panchal.

Publisher Information

Copyright © 2024, **DrMedHealth**.

All rights reserved.

No part of this book may be reproduced, distributed, or transmitted in any form or by any means, including photocopying, recording, or other electronic or mechanical methods, without the prior written permission of the publisher, except in the case of brief quotations used for review purposes or academic references.

Under no circumstances will any blame or legal responsibility be held against the publisher, or author, for any damages, reparation, or monetary loss due to the information contained within this book, either directly or indirectly.

Before reading the book, please read the disclaimer.

For permissions, inquiries, or other correspondence:

drmedhealth.com@gmail.com

For more information, please visit.

www.DrMedHealth.com[1]

Disclaimer

The content of this book is a work of fiction. Names, characters, places, medical scenarios, and incidents are either the product of the author's imagination or are used fictitiously. Any resemblance to actual persons, living or dead, real-life medical events, organizations, or institutions is purely coincidental.

The medical procedures, treatments, and conditions described are for narrative purposes only and should not be interpreted as professional advice. Readers are advised not to use the medical information presented in this book as a substitute

---

1. http://www.DrMedHealth.com

for consulting healthcare professionals or seeking proper medical care.

Neither the author, Dr. Nilesh Panchal, nor the publisher, **DrMedHealth**, assumes any responsibility for actions taken based on the information contained within these novels. Any opinions expressed in the book are solely those of the author and do not represent the views of any affiliated institutions or organizations.

Chapter 1: A Routine Day

The sun broke through the heavy morning fog as Dr. Arjun Verma pulled into the hospital parking lot. Another day awaited him at Pratham Heart Institute, a renowned center for cardiac care in the bustling city of Pune. Dr. Verma had made a name for himself in the world of cardiology—his steady hands and clinical precision had saved countless lives over the years. At forty-five, he had earned the respect of his peers and the trust of his patients. Yet, for him, the heart remained a puzzle that could never be completely solved—a delicate blend of muscle and mystery.

His day began as it always did: a quick scan of the latest medical journals, a strong cup of coffee, and a brief conversation with the residents before heading into his first round of consultations. His office walls were lined with framed certificates, accolades, and photographs of him with grateful patients, a testament to the life he had built. He valued routine—it was comforting in its predictability, providing order in a field where life and death could hinge on the smallest of details.

The morning passed by in a familiar rhythm. A middle-aged woman with arrhythmia. A young athlete recovering from a recent surgery. A grandfather suffering from chronic heart failure. Each case, though challenging, fell neatly into his extensive understanding of the human heart. He prescribed medications, adjusted treatment plans, and offered reassurances, his mind always calculating, always precise.

But then came the patient who would upend the flow of his day—Mr. Ramesh Kulkarni, a man in his early sixties, accompanied by his anxious daughter. They sat opposite Dr. Verma, their faces tense with worry. Mr. Kulkarni's file indicated that he had been experiencing severe chest pain and shortness of breath for weeks, yet his initial tests had come back inconclusive.

"Good morning, Mr. Kulkarni. I understand you've been having some trouble recently?" Dr. Verma began, offering a reassuring smile. He leaned forward, his gaze steady, trained to read the subtle signs of distress in his patients.

"Yes, doctor," Mr. Kulkarni said, his voice strained. "The pain—it feels like a weight on my chest. Sometimes, it's like my heart is skipping beats."

Dr. Verma nodded and glanced through the test results—electrocardiograms, blood work, and a recent echocardiogram. Everything appeared within normal ranges, yet the symptoms persisted. He noticed slight inconsistencies in the heart's rhythm, but nothing that would typically cause such severe discomfort.

He ordered a more detailed examination, guiding Mr. Kulkarni through a stress test. But as he observed the patient struggling on the treadmill, beads of sweat forming on his forehead, Dr. Verma's concern deepened. The heart rate monitor showed irregular fluctuations that didn't match any pattern he had seen before. It was as if the heart was responding to an unseen force, shifting from slow to rapid beats without warning.

"Strange," he muttered under his breath, focusing on the results with a furrowed brow. The symptoms resembled neither a classic case of arrhythmia nor the typical markers of coronary artery disease. Even rarer conditions like Brugada syndrome or hypertrophic cardiomyopathy had been ruled out by prior tests.

After the stress test, Dr. Verma sat back at his desk, flipping through Mr. Kulkarni's records, looking for any missed clue. The silence in the room was thick as he thought through the possibilities. When he couldn't find any rational explanation, he turned to Mr. Kulkarni's daughter.

"Tell me, has your father been under any unusual stress lately? Any significant changes at home or work?" he asked, hoping for some context that might explain the condition.

She shook her head. "No, doctor. Life has been the same. He hasn't had any major stress or changes. And he's always been healthy—he doesn't even smoke or drink."

Dr. Verma's fingers drummed on the edge of his desk as he considered her words. There was something here that eluded him, a piece of the puzzle that didn't fit the usual picture of cardiovascular disease. He knew better than to ignore his instincts—his experience had taught him that the human body could hide secrets even the most advanced tests couldn't detect.

"Well, Mr. Kulkarni," he said, maintaining his composed demeanor, "I'm going to refer you for some advanced imaging tests and a genetic panel, just to be thorough. We'll get to the bottom of this."

Mr. Kulkarni managed a tired smile, grateful for the doctor's persistence, while his daughter clasped his hand with hope. As they left, Dr. Verma leaned back in his chair, still studying the irregular readings on the monitor, feeling the first stirrings of something he hadn't felt in years—curiosity mixed with unease.

After all these years, he had thought he'd seen every twist and turn the heart could take. But this case was different—more elusive, like a shadow that danced just beyond his understanding. Little did he know, the journey that had just begun would take him far beyond the sterile corridors of his hospital, to a place where science and superstition intertwined, and where the answers he sought would challenge everything he believed.

Chapter 2: Whispers of the Unseen

Dr. Arjun Verma sat in the conference room of Pratham Heart Institute, surrounded by a few of his colleagues, each an expert in their respective fields. The table was cluttered with printouts of test results, ECG tracings, and notes from Mr. Kulkarni's recent stress test. Sunlight streamed through the tall windows, but inside, the air felt heavy with unanswered questions.

"Arjun, I've gone through the scans twice, and I can't see anything out of the ordinary," said Dr. Mehta, a renowned electrophysiologist with a penchant for precision. He shuffled through the papers in front of him, his brow furrowed. "The rhythm inconsistencies aren't typical of any known arrhythmia. It's almost like the heart is reacting to something we're not detecting."

Dr. Verma nodded, knowing that Dr. Mehta's skepticism mirrored his own confusion. Next to him, Dr. Rao, a seasoned cardiothoracic surgeon, leaned back in his chair, crossing his arms. "Maybe we're dealing with a new variant of a known condition, or perhaps a psychological factor playing into the physical symptoms," he suggested. "Have you considered referring him for a psychiatric evaluation?"

Dr. Verma shook his head, though he appreciated the suggestion. "It's more than that. Mr. Kulkarni's symptoms are too physical—too real to be merely psychosomatic. And now, I'm starting to see similar symptoms in two other patients. All older, all with the same inexplicable fluctuations in heart rhythm, and none of them have any obvious stressors or lifestyle changes that would account for this."

The room fell silent as the weight of his words settled in. Dr. Mehta flipped through the ECG tracings again, this time more thoughtfully. "If these cases are connected, we need to look for environmental or genetic links. Perhaps something specific to this region?"

"Maybe," Dr. Verma replied, rubbing his temples. "But until I find more concrete evidence, all I have is a pattern that doesn't fit into any of our existing models. I'll keep investigating and let you know if I find anything."

The meeting adjourned with no definitive answers, leaving Dr. Verma feeling more uncertain than before. He returned to his office, but the sense of unease lingered, gnawing at him as he went through the files of the other two patients, trying to find a common thread. Their backgrounds differed—one a retired schoolteacher, the other a local shopkeeper—yet their symptoms mirrored Mr. Kulkarni's: sudden chest pains, erratic heartbeats, and a profound sense of fatigue. Each time he looked for a medical explanation, he hit a wall.

In the days that followed, he conducted more tests, double-checked the data, and even considered reaching out to researchers at other institutes, but nothing pointed to a clear cause. It was as if a ghost was haunting these patients' hearts, something beyond the reach of medicine's logical grasp. Frustration built inside him like pressure in a valve, but he pushed through it, determined to find an answer.

Then, on a rainy Thursday afternoon, Dr. Verma met with Mrs. Savita Patel, an elderly woman in her late seventies, who had been referred to him with similar complaints. She sat across from him in the examination room, her frail hands clasped tightly around a worn wooden mala. Her face was lined with age, but her eyes held a brightness that hinted at a life lived fully, and her sari was a deep shade of maroon, fraying at the edges.

As he reviewed her symptoms, he found himself slipping into a familiar pattern of questioning, but something in her manner made him pause. After discussing her medical history, he noticed her clutching the mala with a sort of desperation.

"You seem worried, Mrs. Patel. Is there something you're not telling me?" Dr. Verma asked gently, setting down her file.

She hesitated, her eyes darting to the closed door of the examination room, as if fearing someone might overhear. After a long pause, she leaned closer, her voice barely a whisper. "Doctor, I don't know if you believe in such things, but... I think my heart troubles are not from this world."

Dr. Verma raised an eyebrow, but he let her continue. "There's an old belief in my village, doctor. They say that when a heart suffers without cause, it is because the spirits of the past have placed a burden upon it."

She paused, gauging his reaction, but when he only nodded, she continued, "Our family comes from a village in the Konkan region, called Devgarh. It's a small place, barely known to the world outside. There is a story, a legend, that has been told for generations... about a curse that was placed on our ancestors long ago."

Dr. Verma tried to maintain his professional demeanor, but curiosity flickered within him. "A curse, you say? What kind of curse?"

"They say," she whispered, clutching the mala tighter, "that many years ago, a healer from our village was wronged. Her heart was broken, and in her grief, she placed a curse on those who had betrayed her. She vowed that their descendants would feel the weight of her suffering in their hearts, that they would carry her pain with every beat."

Her words hung in the air, mingling with the rhythmic tapping of rain against the window. Dr. Verma suppressed a sigh, reminding himself that folklore often filled the gaps left by unexplainable ailments. But as he looked into Mrs. Patel's eyes, he saw genuine fear—a fear that felt almost tangible.

"And you believe this story has something to do with your condition?" he asked, keeping his tone neutral.

"I don't know, doctor," she replied, her voice breaking. "But I have seen it happen before. My own father suffered from a similar affliction—his heart would race and slow without reason, just like mine. And now, it's happening to me. My family believes that the curse is real, that it's come back to claim us."

Dr. Verma leaned back in his chair, absorbing her words. He was a man of science, bound to the rigors of evidence and data, yet he could not deny the unease her story stirred within him. He had encountered patients before who believed in the supernatural, but this felt different—more insistent, more urgent.

"I appreciate you sharing this with me, Mrs. Patel," he said finally, offering her a small smile. "I promise I'll do everything in my power to find a medical explanation for your condition. But for now, let's focus on the tests and see where that leads us."

She nodded, though the look in her eyes told him that she did not expect science to find the answers. As she left, shuffling slowly out of the room, Dr. Verma sat in silence, her words echoing in his mind. A curse, a village, a healer's broken heart... It all seemed too fantastical, too far removed from the world of medicine.

Yet, as he glanced at the files spread across his desk, with their inscrutable data and erratic heart rhythms, he couldn't shake the feeling that perhaps, somewhere in the intersection between myth and medicine, there lay a clue he had yet to uncover.

The rain outside intensified, drumming against the windows in a chaotic rhythm, mirroring the turmoil within him. For the first time in years, he found himself staring into the unknown, where science had no answers and whispers of the unseen lingered just beyond reach.

Chapter 3: The Village of Shadows

The rain had slowed to a gentle drizzle, creating a soft patter against the window of Dr. Verma's study. As he sat at his desk, Mrs. Patel's words echoed in his mind, mingling with the rustling leaves outside. He knew he should focus on the stack of patient records before him, but his thoughts kept drifting back to her story. Devgarh—a name that carried a weight of mystery, tugging at the edges of his curiosity.

Dr. Verma leaned back in his chair, letting the shadows lengthen around him as the day turned into evening. He closed his eyes and allowed himself to imagine the village she had spoken of. In his mind, the fog of time lifted, revealing a place far removed from the city's clamor—a place where whispers carried old secrets, and shadows held onto the past.

The story began centuries ago, in a village nestled deep within the rugged hills of the Konkan region. Devgarh was a place where dense forests met the coastline, where the scent of salt and earth mingled in the air. The villagers lived a simple life, relying on the rhythms of nature—the planting and harvesting, the ebb and flow of the tides. But beneath this simplicity, there lingered an unspoken fear, a tale that had seeped into the very soil of Devgarh.

In those days, the village had a healer named Ahalya, known for her wisdom and her deep connection to the natural world. She was a young woman with a serene presence, someone who could calm the most restless heart with just a touch of her hand. People would travel from distant hamlets to seek her remedies—herbal pastes for wounds, infusions for fevers, and poultices to soothe the aches of the body. Yet, it was her understanding of the heart that made her truly revered.

Ahalya could listen to a heartbeat and know its secrets. She could sense when a heart was weighed down by sorrow or when it beat with the joy of new love. She would say that the heart was like a river, flowing with emotions, and when it was blocked, pain would follow.

But Ahalya's own heart was not untouched by the trials of life. She had fallen in love with a young man from the village, a fisherman named Devan. They spent many evenings by the sea, dreaming of a life together, promising to face whatever challenges lay ahead. Ahalya's heart was full in those days, beating with a rhythm that matched the waves that crashed upon the shore.

Yet fate had other plans. The village elders, wary of Ahalya's growing influence, arranged for Devan to marry the daughter of a wealthy landowner. The decision came like a thunderclap, shattering Ahalya's dreams. She begged Devan to stand by her, to defy the elders, but he bowed to their will, leaving her alone with her grief.

Betrayed and heartbroken, Ahalya retreated to the edge of the village, where the forest grew thick and wild. She refused to see anyone, her once-gentle demeanor replaced by a silence that even the wind dared not disturb. Days turned into weeks, and rumors spread among the villagers. They spoke of strange sounds coming from her hut at night—whispers that carried on the breeze, shadows that moved without form.

Then, one dark evening, the air thick with the promise of rain, Ahalya emerged from her solitude. She stood in the center of the village, her face pale and her eyes hollow, as if the spirit of life had been drained from her. She held a small vial of dark liquid in her hands, a concoction that she claimed would bind her heart's suffering to those who had wronged her.

The villagers gathered around her, some curious, others fearful. Ahalya spoke, her voice carrying a chill that seemed to seep into the ground. "You took my heart and shattered it. Now, my pain shall become yours. As long as this village stands, those who carry the blood of betrayal will know the weight of a broken heart."

With those words, she drank the vial, a bitter smile on her lips, and collapsed to the ground. The villagers rushed to her side, but it was too late—Ahalya was gone. Her body lay cold, but the silence that followed was colder still, a silence that wrapped around the village like a shroud.

For a time, the villagers dismissed her curse as the ramblings of a broken woman. But soon, strange occurrences began to unfold. People in the village started experiencing unexplained chest pains, their hearts racing or slowing without cause. The village healer who succeeded Ahalya found himself unable to explain the symptoms that defied all remedies.

Rumors spread quickly, stories of Ahalya's restless spirit, haunting those who had betrayed her. Families whispered of ancestors who had suddenly fallen ill, their hearts faltering as if in response to an unseen hand. The elders who had forced

Devan into marriage became the first to suffer, their descendants bearing the burden of a mysterious ailment that seemed to pass from one generation to the next.

As the years turned into decades, the story of Ahalya's curse became woven into the fabric of Devgarh's existence. The villagers learned to fear the signs—an unexplained ache, a missed heartbeat, the shadow that seemed to move just beyond the corner of one's vision. They built shrines to appease her spirit, leaving offerings of flowers and incense by the edge of the forest, hoping to ward off her wrath.

But the curse never truly faded. Like an echo, it persisted, its rhythm aligning with the beating of hearts. It became a part of the village's identity, a darkness that clung to their history, casting a shadow over every generation that followed.

As the vision of Devgarh's past faded, Dr. Verma opened his eyes, blinking against the dim light of his study. He let out a slow breath, his heart beating heavily in his chest, as if in response to the story that had come alive in his mind. He found himself wondering whether the ancient healer's curse could be more than just a fable. Could there be a link between Ahalya's story and the strange symptoms he was witnessing in his patients?

It was absurd, of course. He was a man of science, and yet, he couldn't ignore the unease that settled in his chest like a persistent ache. He thought back to Mr. Kulkarni, to Mrs. Patel, to the irregular heart rhythms that defied his understanding. The parallels between the myth and the reality he was facing seemed too close to be a mere coincidence.

Ahalya's story spoke of a heart's suffering, of emotions that could poison the blood, of pain that could pass through generations. And here he was, dealing with a mysterious condition that seemed to do just that—afflicting hearts without any physical explanation. It was as if the curse, real or imagined, had found a new way to manifest in the modern world.

Dr. Verma shook his head, trying to clear the fog of uncertainty that clouded his thoughts. He knew he needed to stay focused on the medical facts, but a part of him couldn't help but wonder if Mrs. Patel's words held a kernel of truth. Perhaps, buried within the folklore of Devgarh, there was a clue that could lead him to the answers he sought.

With a renewed sense of determination, he made a decision. He would dig deeper into the history of the village, search for any records or stories that might provide a link to the symptoms his patients were experiencing. He knew it was a path that many of his colleagues would dismiss as unscientific, but he couldn't ignore the whisper that lingered in his mind, urging him to look beyond the known.

The shadows of Devgarh might hold secrets, and perhaps, just perhaps, the answers to a puzzle that no textbook could solve.

Chapter 4: The Unraveling

Dr. Verma sat at his desk late into the night, poring over stacks of patient files and handwritten notes. His office was dimly lit by the glow of a desk lamp, casting shadows that stretched across the walls like specters from another world. He had been sifting through medical histories, looking for any common thread that might explain the mysterious heart condition plaguing his patients. Yet, time and again, his efforts seemed to yield only more questions.

What he had discovered so far was subtle but intriguing: each of the three patients he had treated, including Mr. Kulkarni and Mrs. Patel, had roots in the Konkan region. While the details of their family histories varied, they all traced their ancestry back to a cluster of remote villages, including one that kept coming up—Devgarh. It was a faint link, but it was the only one he had.

Dr. Verma leaned back, rubbing his tired eyes. He knew that even suggesting a connection between an ancient legend and a modern medical condition would invite ridicule. He could almost hear his colleagues dismissing the idea as a flight of fancy, a distraction from the rigorous search for scientific explanations. But his instincts told him otherwise, and he couldn't shake the nagging feeling that this was more than coincidence.

He spent the next week speaking with his patients, gently probing for details about their family backgrounds. Many were reluctant, viewing the questions as irrelevant, but he managed to gather bits and pieces that filled in the picture. As he cross-referenced the information, he found that some of the affected families had once lived in or near Devgarh before moving to the city. Each family spoke, in hushed tones, of whispers carried through the generations—tales of misfortune that followed those who left the village behind.

Then came the day that shifted everything. It was a quiet morning when Dr. Verma received a call from Mr. Kulkarni's daughter, Maya, asking if she could bring in some of her father's belongings. She sounded anxious, mentioning something she had found among his things that might be of interest.

Later that afternoon, she arrived at the hospital, clutching a small, worn cloth bundle. Her eyes were red, the strain of her father's deteriorating condition evident in her face. She placed the bundle on Dr. Verma's desk, unfolding it with careful hands. Inside lay a small brass pendant, tarnished with age, its intricate engravings barely visible. The pendant was shaped like a heart, but not like any anatomical heart that Dr. Verma had studied. It was more stylized, with symbols that seemed to merge the outline of a heart with patterns resembling veins and roots.

"My father never told me much about this," Maya said, her voice trembling. "I found it in his old belongings, wrapped in a corner of his trunk. When I asked him about it, he said it was something passed down through the family, that it was meant to keep us safe. But when he mentioned it, he seemed... afraid."

Dr. Verma picked up the pendant, feeling the cold weight of it in his hand. He turned it over, noting the faint markings on the back—characters that looked like they belonged to an ancient script, worn smooth over time. The pendant seemed to pulse with a strange energy, as if it held the memories of those who had carried it before.

"Do you know where this came from?" he asked, his mind racing with the implications.

Maya shook her head. "All he said was that it came from our ancestral village, Devgarh. He never spoke of it before he got sick, and I think he thought it might be connected somehow. He wanted me to keep it safe, but I don't know what to make of it."

Dr. Verma's thoughts churned as he placed the pendant back in the cloth. The connection to Devgarh was undeniable now. The pendant, with its mysterious engravings and the unease it seemed to evoke, felt like a bridge between the past and the present—between the folklore he had dismissed and the very real suffering of his patients.

"Thank you for bringing this to me, Maya," he said softly, trying to reassure her. "I'll look into this further, and I promise, we'll do everything we can for your father."

After she left, he held the pendant in his hand, feeling its cold metal against his palm. Could this be a relic from the time of Ahalya, the healer whose curse had lingered over Devgarh's history? He didn't know, but it seemed to carry the weight of untold stories, of lives intertwined with sorrow and hope.

Later that evening, Dr. Verma brought up the topic in a meeting with his colleagues, presenting his findings in a careful, measured way. He described the pendant, the connection to Devgarh, and the patients' shared backgrounds, but he was met with skepticism.

Dr. Mehta furrowed his brow, crossing his arms as he leaned back in his chair. "Arjun, you're seriously suggesting that we're dealing with some kind of... what, a hereditary curse? We're doctors, not archaeologists."

Dr. Rao raised an eyebrow, adding, "Even if there's a common ancestry among the patients, it doesn't explain how this supposed curse could manifest as a heart condition. There must be a genetic explanation, maybe something tied to the region's diet or environment."

Dr. Verma held his ground, trying to keep the frustration out of his voice. "I'm not saying that I believe in curses, but there's something here—something that we don't understand yet. The pendant is a tangible link to the village's past. It might not be medical, but it's cultural, and it's influencing the way these families perceive their illness. It's worth investigating."

Dr. Mehta shook his head, a wry smile on his lips. "You've always had a soft spot for stories, Arjun, but this is a hospital. We need facts, data, not myths."

The conversation ended with a polite but firm reminder to focus on clinical evidence, leaving Dr. Verma to wrestle with his doubts alone. Yet, as he sat in his office, staring at the pendant that seemed to gleam in the dim light, he felt a growing certainty. He knew he couldn't ignore this connection, no matter how intangible it seemed. The answers wouldn't be found in medical textbooks or clinical trials; they lay somewhere in the shadowy space between science and belief.

Dr. Verma's next step was to reach out to a local historian who specialized in the folklore of the Konkan region. He brought the pendant to their meeting, explaining its background and the strange circumstances surrounding his patients.

The historian, an elderly man with thinning white hair and a keen eye for detail, examined the pendant with reverence. "This design is old, very old," he murmured, tracing the worn symbols with his finger. "It's from a time when people believed that objects could hold power, that a part of one's spirit could be bound to something physical."

He paused, glancing up at Dr. Verma with a knowing look. "They say that some healers in those days would create talismans to protect their families. But if Ahalya's story is true, it's possible that such an artifact could carry a different kind of weight—one meant to hold onto pain, to carry a burden through the generations."

Dr. Verma listened, absorbing the implications. "So, you think this could be connected to Ahalya's curse? That it could have... influenced the way these families experience illness?"

The historian shrugged, a small smile playing on his lips. "Science and belief have their own ways of explaining the world. I don't have the answers, Doctor. But sometimes, the lines between what we see and what we feel are not as clear as we'd like them to be."

As he left the historian's office, Dr. Verma felt a sense of urgency building within him. He knew that his next step would be to visit Devgarh, to walk the same paths that Ahalya once walked, and to uncover whatever secrets the village still held. But he also knew that his search would not just be for answers—it would be a journey into the unknown, where logic and superstition intertwined like the tangled roots of an ancient tree.

The pendant, now tucked safely in his pocket, felt heavier than ever. It was a reminder that sometimes, even the heart's mysteries could not be unraveled by reason alone. As he drove home that night, the city lights blurring through the rain-slicked streets, Dr. Verma couldn't shake the feeling that the real story of Devgarh had only just begun to unfold.

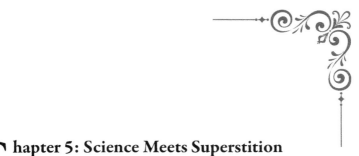

Chapter 5: Science Meets Superstition

Dr. Arjun Verma walked through the polished corridors of Pratham Heart Institute, the pendant weighing heavily in his pocket. The rhythmic beep of monitors and the soft murmur of conversations filled the air, but his mind was elsewhere—far away, in the shadowy alleys of Devgarh and the whispers of an ancient curse. He had become increasingly engrossed in his search for answers, splitting his time between reviewing medical research and exploring the tangled web of stories that stretched back generations. His fascination with the connection between folklore and his patients' mysterious heart condition had begun to raise eyebrows among his colleagues.

It wasn't long before his unorthodox approach caught the attention of the hospital board.

The board meeting was called on a gray, overcast afternoon. As Dr. Verma entered the conference room, he was met with a line of stern faces—Dr. Mehta, the hospital's chief cardiologist, Dr. Rao, the head of surgery, and several members of the administrative board, all seated at a long table. They watched him with expressions that ranged from curiosity to outright skepticism.

"Arjun, take a seat," Dr. Mehta said, gesturing to the empty chair at the head of the table. His tone was polite, but the tension in the room was palpable.

Dr. Verma sat down, clutching his notes. He knew what this meeting was about, and he had prepared himself for it. But as he looked around at the faces of those he had worked alongside for years, he couldn't shake the feeling that he was stepping into a trial rather than a discussion.

"Arjun," Dr. Mehta began, leaning forward, "we've heard from some of the residents that you've been spending a lot of time on these... unconventional theories. Digging into patients' family histories, talking about village legends. We understand your dedication, but we're concerned that this isn't the best use of your time, especially when we have more concrete cases that need your expertise."

Dr. Verma took a deep breath, choosing his words carefully. "I appreciate the concern, Dr. Mehta. But I believe there's a connection here that we haven't explored fully. Yes, it's unconventional, but that doesn't mean it's irrelevant. I've found that each of these patients has roots in the village of Devgarh, a place with a history that might hold clues to their condition."

Dr. Rao raised an eyebrow, crossing his arms. "Clues? You're talking about a curse, Arjun. You're a scientist—surely, you see how this sounds. We can't afford to chase after ghost stories when lives are on the line."

Dr. Verma clenched his jaw, feeling a flash of frustration. "I'm not saying I believe in the supernatural. But there could be a genetic factor at play, something that has been passed down through these families over generations. The folklore could be a reflection of that—a cultural way of explaining a medical phenomenon. I'm exploring all angles, and that includes looking into genetic markers that could be common among the affected patients."

Dr. Mehta sighed, his expression softening slightly. "We know you're doing what you think is best, but you're on a slippery slope, my friend. The hospital's reputation is at stake here, and so is yours. If you want to run genetic tests, fine, but leave the stories out of it. We need science, not superstition."

Dr. Verma met his gaze, his voice steady. "I'm not abandoning science. I'm looking for a way to bridge the gap between what we know and what we don't understand. If that means considering cultural context, then I'm willing to take that risk."

The board members exchanged glances, some nodding slightly, others shaking their heads. Finally, Dr. Mehta leaned back, a resigned look on his face. "All right, Arjun. But be careful. You're walking a fine line, and if you stray too far into... folklore, we won't be able to back you up."

The meeting ended on an uneasy note, with Dr. Verma feeling both isolated and more determined than ever. He left the room with a sense of resolve, knowing that his quest for answers had become more urgent. He couldn't turn back now, not when he was so close to uncovering something that could change the way he understood both medicine and the human heart.

Back in his office, Dr. Verma redoubled his efforts. He poured over medical research, cross-referencing genetic markers that might be linked to cardiac abnormalities. He submitted DNA samples from his patients to a lab, looking for any rare mutations that could explain the erratic heart rhythms. Yet, for every step forward, he encountered dead ends, missing data, and inconclusive results.

Despite the setbacks, he also continued his conversations with the local historian, Mr. Sharma, who had become an unexpected ally in his search for the truth. Mr. Sharma was an elderly man with a passion for preserving the region's oral histories, and he had taken a keen interest in the story of Devgarh and Ahalya's curse.

One evening, they met again in Mr. Sharma's small, book-filled study, the air thick with the smell of old paper and incense. Dr. Verma brought the brass pendant, hoping that the historian could decipher its symbols more thoroughly.

Mr. Sharma examined the pendant under a magnifying glass, his eyes narrowing as he traced the worn engravings. "These symbols are ancient, almost pre-Vedic in origin," he murmured. "They speak of life and death, of the binding between the physical and the spiritual. In those times, people believed that objects like this could channel the energy of those who wore them—whether to protect or to curse."

Dr. Verma listened intently, his skepticism fading as he saw the seriousness in Mr. Sharma's expression. "Do you think Ahalya might have created this? Could it be connected to the curse?"

The historian nodded slowly. "It's possible. If the legend is true, she might have crafted this as a way to bind her pain, to carry her spirit into the generations that followed. In a way, it could be a physical manifestation of her suffering. But whether that suffering has any real power over her descendants is a question only you can answer, Doctor."

Dr. Verma held the pendant in his hand, feeling its cold weight. "I'm looking for a scientific explanation, but every path I take seems to lead back to Devgarh and this curse. It's as if there's a pattern I can't fully see—a rhythm that I'm missing."

Mr. Sharma smiled faintly, leaning back in his chair. "Science and superstition have always been two sides of the same coin, Doctor. They're both ways of trying to understand the world. Perhaps what you're searching for lies somewhere in between."

The words lingered in Dr. Verma's mind as he left the historian's study that night. He drove through the quiet streets, the city lights casting long shadows across the pavement. As he passed by darkened buildings and silent intersections, he felt a growing urgency—a sense that time was running out for his patients, and for him to find the truth.

The next day, he returned to the lab results with renewed focus, searching for any anomalies that could explain the heart condition. He found a minor mutation in a gene related to cardiac rhythm, but it was rare and not conclusively linked to the symptoms his patients were experiencing. It was a clue, but not a definitive answer.

And yet, as he cross-referenced the genetic data with the patients' stories and the folklore of Devgarh, he began to see a possible connection. The genetic mutation, though not fully understood, could have been interpreted as a sign of a "cursed" bloodline by the villagers. What if the ancient healer, Ahalya, had recognized the signs of this condition in her time, interpreting it through the lens of her own suffering? What if her curse was a way of describing a genetic anomaly that science had yet to fully explain?

Dr. Verma knew he had to go further—beyond the boundaries of medicine, beyond the skepticism of his peers, and into the heart of the mystery that tied together the past and the present. As he sat in his office, turning the brass pendant over in his hands, he realized that his journey was no longer just about solving a medical puzzle. It was about confronting the unknown, the spaces where science met superstition, where the heart's secrets lay hidden in the shadows of time.

He made up his mind. He would travel to Devgarh, speak to those who still remembered the stories of Ahalya, and see for himself the place where the curse was born. It was a step that no other doctor would have taken, but he felt that it was the only way forward.

With the pendant tucked into his pocket, Dr. Verma left the hospital that evening, the shadows growing long around him. He had crossed a line, and there would be no turning back. Ahead lay a journey into the unknown, where the past and present intertwined like the tangled roots of an ancient tree. And perhaps, somewhere within those roots, he would find the truth he sought—a truth that lay in the balance between belief and reason, science and the unseen.

Chapter 6: Echoes from the Past

The night was thick with the scent of rain-soaked earth as Dr. Arjun Verma sat in his study, turning the brass pendant over and over in his hands. Outside, a storm brewed, its rumblings in the distance like the heartbeat of the sky, restless and unsteady. It seemed a fitting backdrop for the story that had taken root in his mind—a story of loss, betrayal, and an ancient curse that refused to die. He closed his eyes, allowing himself to be transported back to the village of Devgarh, to the tale of Ahalya that had haunted him since the day Mrs. Patel spoke of the curse.

The story went that Ahalya had once been the heart of Devgarh, a healer whose presence was like a balm to the weary souls of the village. But after Devan's betrayal, when he had chosen another over her under pressure from the village elders, something inside Ahalya shattered. Her laughter, which had once filled the village with warmth, was silenced. Her hands, which had healed so many, now trembled with a pain that no medicine could ease.

She retreated to a hut at the edge of the forest, far from the village's prying eyes. At first, the villagers left her alone, respecting her grief. But as the weeks passed, strange rumors began to spread. Some claimed they heard her weeping at night, her cries carried by the wind. Others spoke of seeing her shadow among the trees, moving with a life of its own, even when she remained inside her hut.

One moonless night, Ahalya emerged from her isolation and walked into the village square, where the elders had gathered to celebrate the upcoming harvest. Her face was pale, almost spectral, her eyes hollow like darkened wells. She carried with her a small vial filled with a dark, thick liquid—her own concoction, brewed from the rare herbs she had once used to heal.

"Do you think you can forget what you've done to me?" she spoke, her voice carrying a bitterness that cut through the festive air. "Do you think my heart is the only one that can break?"

The villagers fell silent, unease rippling through the crowd. Devan, standing among the elders, could not meet her gaze. He had never forgiven himself for what he had done, but he had convinced himself that it was in the past, that Ahalya would eventually forget. But as he looked at her now, he realized how deeply he had underestimated the weight of her sorrow.

Ahalya uncorked the vial and poured its contents onto the earth, the dark liquid soaking into the soil. She whispered words in an ancient dialect, words that none of the villagers could understand, but their meaning was clear. She raised her hand, pointing towards the elders, her expression twisted with pain.

"You took away my joy, my love, my life. Now, my pain will be your burden. As long as Devgarh stands, my suffering will flow through the hearts of those who follow you. It will be passed from one generation to the next, a shadow that will never leave you."

With those words, she collapsed, her body crumpling like a flower wilting under a scorching sun. By the time the villagers reached her, Ahalya was gone, her lifeless eyes staring into the night sky. But the darkness she had invoked lingered in the air, settling into the earth like a lingering echo.

As Dr. Verma opened his eyes, the memory of Ahalya's story left a chill running through him. The tale, though ancient and filled with elements of the supernatural, carried a truth that he could not ignore. It spoke of a pain so deep that it had become a part of the land itself, passed down through the bloodlines of those who had wronged her. He couldn't shake the feeling that there was a connection between this story and the unexplained heart conditions he had been encountering.

But Ahalya's curse was just a story, he reminded himself, a way for the villagers to explain the inexplicable. And yet, as he stared at the brass pendant on his desk, its strange symbols glinting in the lamplight, he wondered if there might be more to it. What if Ahalya's words had been an attempt to articulate something real, something she had sensed but could not explain in the terms of her time?

The more he thought about it, the more he realized that he couldn't solve this mystery from the confines of his office. He needed to see Devgarh for himself, to walk through its streets, to speak to those who still remembered the stories, and to uncover whatever secrets the village still held. He knew it was a decision that would invite criticism from his colleagues, that his obsession with the curse had already strained his reputation. But he couldn't ignore the pull he felt towards the village, as if it were calling to him across time.

That evening, Dr. Verma discussed his decision with his family over dinner. His wife, Priya, listened with a worried expression, her hands resting gently on the edge of the dining table.

"Arjun, I understand that you want to help your patients, but this... this is starting to sound like an obsession," Priya said, her voice tight with concern. "Devgarh is just a village, and the curse is just a story. What if you go there and find nothing?"

Dr. Verma sighed, pushing his half-eaten food aside. "I know it sounds irrational, Priya. But I have this feeling—this sense that there's something important I'm missing. I've run every test, followed every lead, but none of it makes sense. What if the answers aren't in the data? What if they're in the history, in the stories?"

His teenage son, Aarav, who had been listening quietly, looked up from his phone, curiosity lighting up his face. "You're saying there's a real curse, Dad? Like, magic and stuff?"

Dr. Verma smiled faintly at his son's excitement. "No, Aarav, not magic. But sometimes, stories hold truths that science hasn't discovered yet. I'm trying to find out what's real and what's not."

Priya reached out and placed her hand over his. "Just promise me you'll be careful. We need you here, Arjun. Your patients need you."

He squeezed her hand, nodding. "I promise. I'll be back soon. But I have to see this through."

The next day, at the hospital, Dr. Verma faced a wave of skepticism from his colleagues when they learned of his plan to visit Devgarh. Dr. Mehta was especially vocal, catching him in the hallway as he packed up his bag.

"Arjun, you're really going through with this?" Dr. Mehta asked, his tone hovering between disbelief and frustration. "You're abandoning your practice to chase after a village ghost story?"

Dr. Verma met his gaze calmly. "I'm not abandoning my practice, Mehta. I'm following a lead. If I find nothing, I'll come back and focus on the lab results. But if there's even a chance that Devgarh holds the answers, I owe it to my patients to explore it."

Dr. Mehta shook his head, exhaling sharply. "You're a good doctor, Arjun, one of the best. But don't let this ruin everything you've built. You're risking your credibility—"

"And if I'm right, I could save lives," Dr. Verma interjected, his voice firm. "If this was just about me, I'd let it go. But it's not. It's about my patients, and I won't give up on them."

Dr. Mehta stared at him for a moment, then sighed, stepping back. "Fine. Just... be careful. Don't get lost in those shadows."

Dr. Verma nodded, appreciating the concern hidden beneath his colleague's harsh words. As he walked away, he felt a mixture of apprehension and determination settle over him. He knew that his journey to Devgarh would be fraught with uncertainty, that he might face more questions than answers.

But as he left the hospital that evening, the pendant clutched in his hand like a key to a door that had long been sealed, he felt a strange sense of purpose guiding his steps. It was as if the echoes of the past were calling out to him, urging him to unravel the mystery that had lingered in the shadows of time.

The road ahead was uncertain, but he was ready to face whatever truths lay hidden in the village where Ahalya's curse had been born. He knew that the journey would take him far beyond the world of modern medicine, into a place where science and superstition met, where the heart's secrets whispered through the wind and the soil. And perhaps, somewhere within that ancient village, he would find the answers that had eluded him for so long.

Chapter 7: Journey to the Unknown

Dr. Arjun Verma steered his car through the winding, narrow roads that led into the heart of Devgarh. The journey had taken him far from the bustling city of Pune, through rolling hills and dense forests where the trees seemed to whisper ancient secrets. As he drove deeper into the Konkan region, the air grew thick with humidity, carrying the earthy scent of rain-soaked leaves. It felt like crossing a threshold into another world—one where time moved at a slower pace, and the boundary between the past and present blurred.

He arrived at the village as the sun began to sink behind the hills, casting long shadows across the fields. Devgarh was nestled in a valley, its houses clustered together like a huddle of secrets. The village seemed untouched by modernity; its narrow lanes were lined with thatched huts and crumbling stone walls covered in creeping vines. A small temple stood at the village's center, its bell tolling softly as evening prayers began. The sound echoed through the empty streets, mingling with the distant calls of birds settling in for the night.

Dr. Verma parked his car near the temple and stepped out, feeling the eyes of the villagers upon him. A few men and women had gathered by a well, their conversations fading into silence as they noticed the stranger in their midst. He felt their suspicion prickling at his skin, like a distant hum he couldn't ignore.

"Namaste," he greeted them, offering a polite nod, but the villagers only exchanged wary glances. A middle-aged man with a weathered face and a turban tied tightly around his head stepped forward, eyeing Dr. Verma with open distrust.

"You are not from here, Doctor," the man said, his voice thick with the local accent. "What brings you to Devgarh?"

Dr. Verma held out his hands in a gesture of peace. "I'm here to learn about the history of this place. Some of my patients are connected to Devgarh, and I believe the stories from your village might help me understand their condition."

The man frowned, his brow furrowing deeply. "Stories? What stories? We are simple people, Doctor. We don't have anything to share with outsiders."

Dr. Verma knew he was treading on delicate ground. He chose his words carefully. "I've heard of Ahalya, the healer who lived here long ago. Some say her curse still lingers. I want to understand her story, not as a doctor, but as someone who respects the past."

At the mention of Ahalya's name, a hush fell over the small gathering. The man stiffened, glancing around as if the very air might betray their conversation. He leaned in closer, his voice dropping to a harsh whisper. "We do not speak of Ahalya. Her spirit still walks among these hills. If you value your safety, you will leave this place."

Before Dr. Verma could respond, the man turned on his heel and walked away, motioning for the others to follow. The villagers scattered, their footsteps fading into the narrow alleys, leaving Dr. Verma standing alone under the growing shadows. He felt a shiver run down his spine, but he pushed it aside.

He hadn't come all this way to be turned back by fear and superstition.

Dr. Verma made his way to a small guesthouse at the edge of the village, where he had arranged to stay for the duration of his visit. The guesthouse was a modest structure, its walls adorned with faded murals of mythological scenes. The owner, an elderly woman with cataract-clouded eyes, led him to a room with a simple cot and a wooden desk. She said little, but as she handed him the key, she murmured, "Devgarh is a place where the past never dies, Doctor. Be careful where you tread."

That night, as he lay on the creaking cot, listening to the nocturnal sounds of the forest outside, Dr. Verma thought of the villagers' reaction. They feared Ahalya's story, but that fear seemed to be more than just superstition—it was as if the memory of the healer had become a living presence, woven into the fabric of the village itself. He knew that if he wanted answers, he would have to find a way to unravel the truth hidden within their silence.

The next morning, Dr. Verma rose early and walked through the village, tracing the paths that Ahalya might have walked centuries ago. He passed by the temple and found his way to a small, dusty library housed in a building that seemed to have withstood the wear of time. The librarian, a frail man with a tuft of white hair and a hesitant smile, eyed him curiously when he introduced himself.

"You are looking for records about Ahalya?" the librarian asked, his voice barely more than a rasp. "Few people care about those old stories anymore. But there are some books and journals that might interest you. They speak of the healer, though not many like to read them."

Dr. Verma followed the librarian into the dimly lit room lined with shelves that bowed under the weight of ancient volumes. He spent hours combing through crumbling journals and yellowed manuscripts, some of which were written in the old Marathi script, barely legible with age. As he read, he came across accounts that mirrored the symptoms of his patients—descriptions of villagers who had suffered from unexplained chest pains, erratic heartbeats, and a sense of unease that seemed to linger in their bloodlines.

One entry caught his attention. It was from a journal dated over a century ago, written by a village elder who described the fear that had gripped Devgarh after Ahalya's death. According to the elder, descendants of the elders who had betrayed Ahalya had suffered from a "curse of the heart," a shadow that fell upon those whose families had once wronged her. The symptoms were described in eerie detail—palpitations, sudden fatigue, a heaviness in the chest that no remedy could ease.

Dr. Verma's pulse quickened as he read the words, his mind drawing connections between these accounts and the condition afflicting his patients. It was as if the stories of Ahalya's curse had preserved a memory of an inherited ailment, a legacy that had persisted through the generations, hidden beneath layers of myth and belief.

That evening, as the sun dipped below the horizon, Dr. Verma wandered through the village, lost in thought. He came upon an old shrine at the edge of the forest, where incense and marigold garlands had been placed as offerings to a weathered idol. He was about to turn back when he noticed a figure standing among the shadows—an old man, dressed in a simple white dhoti, his hair long and unkempt.

The man's presence seemed almost ethereal, as if he had stepped out from another time. He met Dr. Verma's gaze with eyes that seemed to hold an ancient sadness, the lines of his face carved deep by years and secrets.

"You are the doctor who seeks Ahalya's story," the old man said, his voice like the creak of old wood. "But some stories do not wish to be found."

Dr. Verma felt a shiver run through him. "I only want to understand, to find the truth behind what has been happening to my patients. You know something, don't you?"

The old man smiled faintly, his expression inscrutable. "The truth is like a shadow, Doctor—it changes with the light. What you seek may not bring you peace."

Dr. Verma stepped closer, desperation tinging his voice. "Please, if you know anything that could help me, tell me. My patients are suffering."

The old man studied him for a long moment, then turned his gaze towards the forest. "Ahalya's pain lingers here, in the earth, in the air. It has seeped into the hearts of those who bear her memory. But there is more to the story than you will find in books or records. If you wish to understand, you must face the place where her spirit rests."

He gestured towards the dark line of trees, where the forest thickened into a tangle of shadows. "Beyond those trees lies the hut where Ahalya lived and died. It is a place that holds echoes of her last breath, her final curse. But beware, Doctor, for those who seek her spirit do not always return the same."

Dr. Verma felt a chill settle in his bones, but he nodded, determination tightening his resolve. "Thank you," he said, but when he turned back towards the shrine, the old man was gone, leaving only the rustling of the leaves and the distant call of night birds.

He stood there for a moment, staring into the forest, the old man's words echoing in his mind. The journey ahead would be dangerous, but he felt that he was closer than ever to uncovering the truth. Somewhere in the shadows of Devgarh, among the tangled roots of myth and memory, lay the answers he sought. And no matter what he found, he knew he could not turn back now.

With a final glance towards the forest, Dr. Verma turned and made his way back to the guesthouse, his mind set on the path that lay ahead. The night seemed darker than before, the air heavy with the promise of revelation and the weight of the past.

Chapter 8: A Silent Heart

The rain beat against the windowpanes of Dr. Arjun Verma's guesthouse room in Devgarh, as he pored over the notes he had taken during his time in the village. His mind was full of half-formed theories and fragments of old stories, but he knew that whatever truth he sought lay hidden within the echoes of the past. Just as he was about to turn in for the night, his phone rang, the sharp sound cutting through the steady rhythm of the rain.

It was Maya, the daughter of his patient, Mr. Kulkarni. Her voice trembled on the other end, choked with panic. "Dr. Verma, it's my father—his condition... it's worsened. He's in the ICU, and the doctors say... they say there's nothing more they can do."

Dr. Verma felt a chill seep through him, his mind snapping back to the reality he had left behind in the city. "I'm coming back," he said, his voice tight with urgency. "Stay with him. I'll be there as soon as I can."

He gathered his things with a sense of dread settling in his chest, the pendant slipping into his pocket like a weight he couldn't shake. As he drove back to Pune through the storm-lashed roads, he couldn't silence the fear gnawing at his thoughts—what if he was already too late?

By the time Dr. Verma arrived at the hospital, the night had given way to the pale gray of dawn. He rushed through the sterile corridors to the ICU, but as he reached the room, the sight that greeted him made his breath catch. Maya sat beside her father's bed, her face buried in her hands, while the machines that had once monitored his heart lay silent, the lines on the screen flat and unyielding.

Dr. Verma's heart sank as he approached, placing a gentle hand on Maya's shoulder. She looked up at him, her eyes red with tears, her voice barely more than a whisper. "He's gone, Doctor. He just... slipped away. They said his heart simply... stopped."

Dr. Verma felt a deep ache settle into his bones, a sense of failure that cut deeper than he had expected. He had hoped to find answers before it came to this, to unravel the mystery that had claimed Mr. Kulkarni's life. But now, all he had were questions that circled back to the same enigma—Ahalya's curse, the strange genetic markers, and the unexplained heart rhythms that defied everything he knew about medicine.

He stood in the dimly lit room, watching the lifeless form of a man who had become more than just a patient to him. A man whose suffering had driven him to seek out a village's secrets, to confront the line between science and superstition. And now, that line felt thinner than ever.

In the days that followed Mr. Kulkarni's death, Dr. Verma immersed himself in the data he had collected from the village and his patients. But the pressure had mounted—Maya's grief-stricken face haunted him, and the hospital board's warnings echoed in his ears. He knew that he couldn't afford to fail again.

As he reviewed the environmental factors surrounding Devgarh, a new pattern began to emerge. He noticed that the soil and water in the region had high levels of certain trace minerals—minerals that could, in high concentrations, affect the heart's electrical conduction system. He cross-referenced this with medical journals and found studies linking exposure to these minerals with irregular heart rhythms and cardiovascular stress.

The pieces of the puzzle began to align in his mind. The villagers of Devgarh, those who had lived and worked the land for generations, might have been exposed to these environmental factors, causing subtle changes in their bodies. A genetic predisposition could have made certain families more susceptible to these effects, leading to the condition that had plagued his patients—symptoms that the villagers, without the language of science, had explained as a curse.

Yet, the story of Ahalya and her curse seemed to mirror these findings too closely for comfort. It was as if the folklore had encoded a memory of the suffering, preserving it through myth even as the real cause slipped through the grasp of knowledge.

Dr. Verma knew he had to return to Devgarh, to speak with the villagers again, this time with the newfound understanding that linked their stories to his patients' suffering. When he arrived, the mood of the village had shifted. Word had spread that the city doctor had not given up his search, that he had even faced loss in his pursuit of the truth. The villagers, who had once regarded him with suspicion, now watched him with a mixture of curiosity and grudging respect.

He went to the village square, where a small crowd had gathered—men and women who had known Ahalya's story from childhood, who had whispered her name as if afraid of summoning her spirit. The old librarian, the shopkeeper, the farmer—each had stories to share, fragments of a history that had been passed down in hushed voices.

One by one, the villagers spoke of family members who had suffered from "the burden of the heart," of ancestors who had died suddenly, clutching their chests. They spoke of the unease that seemed to settle in their bones, the way their hearts would race at night as if in response to an unseen force. The stories varied in detail, but a common thread ran through them all—a belief that their suffering was tied to the land, to the curse that Ahalya had left behind.

As Dr. Verma listened, he felt a strange sense of validation. The symptoms they described matched those of his patients—irregular heartbeats, unexplained chest pain, a sense of heaviness that no medicine could alleviate. But while his patients had come to him seeking scientific explanations, the villagers had framed their suffering in the language of spirits and curses.

It was the elderly librarian who spoke last, his voice low and weary with age. "You came here looking for a story, Doctor, but you have found a truth that we have carried for too long. Ahalya's curse was never just about spirits or vengeance. It was about the way this place holds onto us, how it shapes the blood that flows through our veins. Perhaps she understood more than we give her credit for."

Dr. Verma nodded slowly, absorbing the weight of the words. "Maybe she did. And maybe her story was her way of warning us, of telling us what she couldn't explain."

The librarian nodded, a faint smile playing at the corners of his lips. "You are the first outsider to listen. Perhaps that will make a difference."

That night, as Dr. Verma returned to the guesthouse, he felt the weight of a revelation settling over him. He had found the link between the past and the present—between the folklore that spoke of Ahalya's curse and the science that traced the condition to genetic and environmental factors. It was not a curse in the sense that the villagers believed, but a legacy of suffering carried through the land and the people who had lived on it.

But as he lay awake, listening to the rustle of the trees and the distant call of night birds, he knew that his work was not yet done. He still needed to find a way to turn this knowledge into a treatment that could help his patients. He had to convince the hospital board, to show them that the connection between Devgarh's history and the present-day affliction was real.

And above all, he had to come to terms with the realization that sometimes, the stories people told to make sense of their suffering held more truth than science could explain. The heart, he had learned, was more than just a muscle—it was a vessel of memory, a keeper of secrets that spanned centuries.

As he drifted into an uneasy sleep, the rain began to fall again, washing over the village like a cleansing tide. And somewhere in the shadows beyond the guesthouse, where the forest grew thick and ancient, he thought he heard the faint echo of a woman's voice—soft, sorrowful, and full of secrets yet to be uncovered.

Chapter 9: Breaking Boundaries

Dr. Arjun Verma sat in the dim light of the guesthouse, his desk cluttered with old journals, medical records, and notes from his time in Devgarh. His mind buzzed with the fragments of stories he had gathered from the villagers and the medical data that had begun to take shape. But there was something else—a piece of folklore that had surfaced in his conversations with the villagers, one that spoke of an ancient herbal remedy used by Ahalya herself. It was said to soothe the "burning heart," a phrase the villagers used to describe the mysterious condition that had plagued their families for generations.

He had first heard of the remedy from the old librarian, who mentioned it almost as an afterthought, speaking of a plant that grew deep in the forest surrounding the village. "They say Ahalya would brew a tea from its leaves," the librarian had said, a wistful note in his voice. "It could calm the heart, ease the pain. But no one has used it for many years. The knowledge was lost when she died."

Dr. Verma's curiosity had been piqued, and he had spent hours digging through the old records in the village library. Finally, he came across a tattered manuscript, its pages yellowed and brittle. The text, written in a dialect that was difficult to decipher, described a plant known as *hridya shanta*, meaning "heart's peace." It spoke of its use as a tonic to stabilize irregular heart rhythms and alleviate chest pain, passed down through the village's healers long before modern medicine reached Devgarh.

The plant's description matched a species he had encountered only once before—a rare herb that grew in the high-altitude forests of the Western Ghats. But scientific studies on its properties were scarce, and no modern research had verified its effects on heart conditions.

As he read through the manuscript, a question gnawed at him—could this ancient remedy hold the key to treating the condition that had eluded his understanding? It was a thought that both excited and unsettled him, pushing him into a space where science and tradition seemed to converge.

Returning to Pune, Dr. Verma couldn't shake the idea from his mind. He took samples of the herb, analyzing its chemical compounds in the hospital's lab. He discovered that the plant contained alkaloids that could potentially act on the heart's calcium channels, a mechanism similar to some modern anti-arrhythmic drugs. The herb's properties seemed to align with the effects described in the village stories, offering a possible explanation for why Ahalya might have believed it could heal the afflicted.

But as he dug deeper into the science, Dr. Verma found himself grappling with an ethical dilemma. Incorporating a traditional remedy into modern treatment would be controversial, especially without the rigorous trials that were required for new medications. His colleagues at the hospital would be skeptical—at best, they would dismiss it as unproven folklore; at worst, they would accuse him of abandoning the principles of evidence-based medicine.

Dr. Mehta had already expressed his doubts about Dr. Verma's "adventures into folklore," as he put it, during their last meeting. And the hospital board was watching him closely, wary of any further deviations from conventional practice. But with Mr. Kulkarni's death weighing heavily on him, and the prospect of more patients suffering the same fate, Dr. Verma knew that he couldn't dismiss the possibility of a new approach—no matter how unconventional it seemed.

One evening, as he sat in his office, staring at the herb samples under the lab's fluorescence, Priya called him. Her voice was soft, filled with concern. "Arjun, you've been spending so much time at the hospital lately. Is everything okay? I feel like you're carrying a burden you're not sharing with me."

Dr. Verma hesitated, the weight of his thoughts pressing down on him. He wanted to tell her about the herb, about the strange connection he had found between Ahalya's remedy and his patients' condition. But he feared her reaction, just as he feared the reaction of his colleagues. "I'm just... trying to find a new approach, Priya," he said finally, keeping his voice steady. "Something that might make a difference."

"You always do what you believe is right, Arjun. Just make sure you don't lose yourself in the process."

Her words lingered in his mind long after the call ended, but they didn't dissuade him from his path. He knew that he couldn't afford to turn away from a potential breakthrough, not when lives were at stake.

A week later, his persistence bore fruit. Dr. Verma's lab analysis revealed a previously unclassified genetic mutation in the DNA of his patients. The mutation was subtle, a variation in a gene that regulated the heart's electrical impulses. It affected the way calcium ions moved in and out of heart cells, disrupting the heart's ability to maintain a steady rhythm.

When he cross-referenced this finding with the genetic samples he had taken from the villagers in Devgarh, he found the same mutation present in several of their bloodlines—families who had been connected to the village for generations. It was as if the mutation had traveled through the ages, woven into the fabric of their DNA, echoing the legend of Ahalya's curse.

Dr. Verma sat back in his chair, staring at the results on his computer screen, a mixture of awe and disbelief washing over him. He had finally found a tangible link between the genetic condition and the folklore that had surrounded Devgarh for centuries. Ahalya's curse, it seemed, was a story that had encoded a real medical condition, a way for the villagers to make sense of a suffering that they could not explain.

But there was more—Dr. Verma's analysis suggested that the alkaloids in the *hridya shanta* herb might counteract the effects of the mutation, helping to stabilize the calcium channels and restore normal heart function. It was a hypothesis that would have to be tested, but it held a promise that he had not found in any modern medication.

He knew that presenting this idea to the hospital board would be a battle, but it was one he was ready to fight. If there was even a chance that this ancient remedy could bring relief to his patients, he owed it to them to try.

The next morning, Dr. Verma called a meeting with the hospital's cardiology team. He presented his findings, showing them the genetic link he had discovered and the potential role of the *hridya shanta* herb in stabilizing the heart's rhythm.

As he expected, the reaction was mixed. Dr. Mehta, sitting at the head of the table, frowned deeply. "Arjun, you're suggesting using an untested herb on patients. This goes against every protocol we have in place. It's too risky, too unproven."

"I know it's unconventional," Dr. Verma replied, his voice steady. "But the genetic evidence is there. This mutation is unique, and we don't have any standard treatments that address it directly. The herb could offer a solution—if we study it carefully, if we run controlled trials. I'm not asking for blind acceptance, but for the chance to explore this possibility."

Dr. Rao, who had been listening with a skeptical expression, leaned forward. "Let's say we allow this—how do you plan to move forward? How do you justify this to the families?"

Dr. Verma met his gaze, the weight of responsibility settling into his words. "I will explain everything to them—what we know, what we don't know, and the risks involved. I'll give them the choice. But I believe that if Ahalya's remedy holds even a fraction of the potential I've seen, it's worth pursuing."

The room fell silent as the doctors exchanged glances. After a long pause, Dr. Mehta sighed, rubbing his temples. "You've always been stubborn, Arjun. You've got three months. If you can produce preliminary results—something that justifies your claims—then we'll discuss moving forward. But don't expect anyone to make this easy for you."

Dr. Verma nodded, a sense of determination settling over him. "Thank you. I won't waste this opportunity."

As he left the meeting, the weight of the challenge ahead pressed down on him, but there was a spark of hope in his chest that hadn't been there before. He had crossed a boundary, stepping into a space where science met tradition, where the stories of the past held the keys to the future.

And as he began the process of testing the ancient remedy, he couldn't help but think that Ahalya herself might have understood what he was trying to do—that her whispers through the centuries had guided him to this moment, where healing was possible, even if it came wrapped in the mysteries of myth.

Chapter 10: Descent into Darkness

The humid air of Devgarh was thick with tension as Dr. Arjun Verma walked through the village streets, his mind weighed down by the challenges ahead. The villagers had started to talk—rumors of the city doctor experimenting with Ahalya's ancient remedies had spread like wildfire. Some saw his efforts as a sign of hope, a chance to heal the wounds that had haunted their families for generations. But others, especially the elders who clung tightly to their traditions, viewed his actions with suspicion and fear.

As he made his way to the small clinic he had set up in the village, he caught snippets of conversations drifting on the breeze. Voices lowered to whispers when they saw him approach, their words carrying both curiosity and wariness.

"Can he really lift the curse?"

"He's meddling with things he doesn't understand..."

"If Ahalya's spirit is disturbed, what will become of us?"

Dr. Verma tried to ignore the murmurs, but they burrowed into his thoughts, sowing seeds of doubt. He knew he was treading dangerous ground, walking the line between science and belief. His work with the *hridya shanta* herb had shown promise—he had seen slight improvements in his patients' heart rhythms, enough to warrant cautious optimism. But the opposition from some villagers had grown louder, fueled by fear that his interference might provoke Ahalya's spirit, rekindling the ancient curse that still haunted their lives.

It all came to a head one sweltering afternoon when a group of village elders confronted him outside the clinic. Led by the same man who had warned him upon his arrival—Ramdas, the self-appointed guardian of tradition—they stood in a tight cluster, blocking his path.

"Doctor, we have allowed you to stay here, even to use our stories and our herbs," Ramdas said, his tone edged with accusation. "But you are crossing a line. Ahalya's curse is not something you can cure with your medicines. It is tied to our blood, our land. If you tamper with her legacy, you put all of us at risk."

Dr. Verma met Ramdas's gaze, frustration bubbling beneath the surface. "I understand your concerns, Ramdas. But this curse—it's a genetic condition, a result of factors that we can address if we work together. Ahalya's story might have preserved the memory of this illness, but we have the tools to treat it now. I am not dismissing your beliefs—I'm trying to find a way to honor them while helping your people."

Ramdas's expression darkened, his hands clenched at his sides. "You think you can understand Ahalya's pain? Her suffering? This is not just about science. It is about a wound that has festered for generations. If you disturb that wound, it will not be only you who suffers the consequences."

Dr. Verma opened his mouth to respond, but before he could speak, he felt a sharp pang in his chest—a sudden, crushing tightness that made him gasp for breath. He staggered, clutching at the front of his shirt, his vision swimming with black spots.

"Doctor, are you all right?" one of the younger villagers called out, rushing to his side, but Dr. Verma could barely hear him over the roaring in his ears. He felt his pulse hammering wildly, as if his heart had turned traitor, slipping into the same erratic rhythm that he had seen in his patients.

For a moment, the world around him blurred, and he thought he saw a shadow flickering at the edge of his vision—a dark figure, standing among the trees, watching him with eyes that glinted like embers. He blinked, and the shadow was gone, leaving only the concerned faces of the villagers and the oppressive heat of the afternoon.

Dr. Verma forced himself to steady his breathing, the pain in his chest subsiding as quickly as it had come. He straightened, wiping sweat from his brow, and gave a shaky nod. "I... I'm fine. Just a bit of dizziness."

But as he met Ramdas's gaze, he saw a knowing look in the elder's eyes, a glimmer of grim satisfaction. "You see, Doctor? Even you cannot escape Ahalya's reach. She is reminding you that her spirit is not to be trifled with."

Dr. Verma said nothing, his mind reeling with the implications of what had just happened. He knew that the episode could have been a result of exhaustion or stress, but it had felt different—strangely personal, as if the curse that had plagued his patients was reaching out to touch him as well.

That night, Dr. Verma lay awake in his room, staring at the dark ceiling, his thoughts spiraling through fear and uncertainty. He tried to convince himself that what he had experienced was just a coincidence, a product of his overworked mind. But he couldn't ignore the lingering ache in his chest, or the memory of the shadow that had seemed to watch him from the trees.

He rose from his bed, drawn to the pendant that lay on the desk. He picked it up, feeling the cool metal against his palm, and slipped it into his pocket. Without thinking, he left the guesthouse and walked into the night, his feet carrying him down the path that led to the edge of the forest.

The moon cast pale light through the branches, illuminating a narrow trail that wound deeper into the woods. Dr. Verma followed the path until he reached the clearing where the shrine to Ahalya stood, a place where villagers left offerings to appease her spirit. He stood before the weathered idol, the pendant clutched tightly in his hand, and called out into the darkness.

"If you are still here, Ahalya... if your spirit lingers in this place, I need to understand. What is this curse you have left behind? What do you want from us?"

For a long moment, there was only silence, broken by the rustling of leaves and the distant hoot of an owl. But then, from the shadows, a figure emerged—the same old man who had spoken to him near the shrine weeks before, his white dhoti fluttering like a specter's shroud in the night breeze.

"You return, Doctor," the old man said, his voice low and grave. "But do you truly wish to know the answers you seek?"

Dr. Verma swallowed hard, the weight of his uncertainty pressing down on him. "I don't know what I believe anymore. I've seen things that defy logic, felt things I can't explain. If you know something—anything—please, tell me."

The old man approached, his face lined with shadows. He reached out and touched the pendant that Dr. Verma held, his fingers tracing the worn symbols. "This is a key, Doctor. Ahalya poured her grief into this land, into these people, but it was never just a curse. It was a way to hold onto what she had lost—to bind her pain to the soil, to the blood of those who remained."

He paused, his eyes reflecting the dim glow of the moon. "When she spoke of the heart that would suffer, she meant more than just the body. She meant the spirit, the legacy of sorrow that would be carried through the generations. But she also left behind a way to heal that wound—a way to remember her without being consumed by her grief. That is what you hold in your hand."

Dr. Verma's mind raced, the old man's words sinking into the depths of his thoughts. "You mean... the herb, the stories, they were meant to teach the villagers how to live with this condition? To find a balance between the past and the present?"

The old man nodded, his expression inscrutable. "But they forgot, over time. They turned the memory into fear, the remedy into a taboo. And so, the suffering continued, until you came to ask the questions they had buried."

Dr. Verma felt a sense of clarity settle over him, like a breeze clearing the fog that had clouded his mind. He understood now—Ahalya's curse had been a way for her to keep her memory alive, a story that had twisted into something darker when its meaning was lost. But within that story lay the knowledge that could bridge the gap between tradition and science.

He turned to the old man, a new determination in his voice. "If there's a way to break this cycle, to help the villagers and my patients, I need to try. But I can't do it alone."

The old man's expression softened, and for the first time, a faint smile touched his lips. "You are not alone, Doctor. Ahalya's spirit will guide you, as it has guided you here. The rest is up to you."

With those words, the old man stepped back into the shadows, his figure dissolving into the night. Dr. Verma stood alone in the clearing, the pendant warm in his hand, a sense of resolve burning in his chest. He knew that the journey ahead would be difficult—that he would face resistance from those who feared change and from those who doubted his methods.

But he also knew that he had found the path he was meant to walk—a path that wound through the past and into the future, where the stories of a village and the science of a doctor could meet and become something new. And as he made his way back to the guesthouse, the forest closing around him like the pages of a forgotten book, he felt a strange peace settle over his heart, even as the darkness lingered on the edges of his vision.

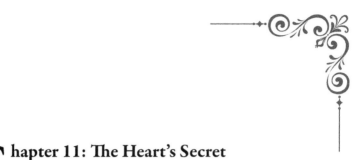

Chapter 11: The Heart's Secret

Dr. Arjun Verma sat in his makeshift lab in the village guesthouse, surrounded by stacks of research papers, genetic test results, and a small vial of crushed *hridya shanta* leaves. The air was thick with the smell of rain, mingling with the earthy scent of the herb that lay spread out before him. He had spent weeks poring over the data, testing and retesting his theories, searching for the link that would bring his understanding of Ahalya's curse into the realm of medical science.

And finally, it was there—a breakthrough that shone like a beam of light through the shadows of uncertainty. The curse, the stories, and the mysterious symptoms that had plagued generations of villagers and his patients were all tied to a rare genetic mutation.

The mutation, as he had suspected, affected a specific gene that regulated calcium ion channels in the heart. The villagers' exposure to certain minerals in the soil and water of Devgarh had exacerbated the condition, triggering irregular heart rhythms and unexplained chest pains. The genetic trait itself wasn't deadly, but in combination with environmental stressors, it created a perfect storm that manifested as the erratic heart conditions he had witnessed.

But it wasn't just the scientific discovery that filled him with hope. His analysis of the *hridya shanta* herb had revealed that its alkaloids acted as a natural calcium channel stabilizer, similar to medications used in modern cardiology. It didn't eliminate the condition, but it could temper its effects, providing a natural balance to the disrupted heart rhythms. It was as if the herb and the condition had evolved together, intertwined through the centuries—nature offering a solution to the very problem it had created.

Dr. Verma stared at the results, feeling a sense of awe and relief wash over him. It was a revelation that merged the threads of science and tradition, connecting Ahalya's ancient knowledge with the tools of modern medicine. He realized now that the curse, as the villagers called it, was never just about supernatural punishment—it was a way for Ahalya to pass down the knowledge she had gathered, to warn and protect those who would come after her.

With this discovery, Dr. Verma set to work, developing a treatment plan that blended the scientific rigor of modern medicine with the wisdom hidden in the folklore of Devgarh. He carefully crafted dosages of the *hridya shanta* extract, supplementing them with low-dose beta blockers and anti-arrhythmic medications. His goal was to stabilize the heart rhythms while minimizing side effects, allowing the herb to support the heart's natural balance.

It wasn't a cure, but it was a path to managing the condition—a way for those affected to live without the constant fear of sudden episodes, without the shadow of Ahalya's curse looming over them.

Convincing the villagers to accept the new treatment plan, however, proved to be a different challenge. Dr. Verma called a gathering in the village square, inviting everyone to hear his findings. The crowd that gathered was filled with wary faces—elders clutching their malas, young mothers holding their children close, and Ramdas, the village guardian, standing with arms crossed at the back of the group.

Dr. Verma stood before them, his notes in hand, but he spoke without reading from them, allowing his words to flow from the heart. "I know that many of you have lived your whole lives fearing Ahalya's curse. You've seen your families suffer, watched as each generation faced the same pain. But today, I want to share with you what I have learned."

He explained the genetic mutation he had discovered, using simple words to describe how it affected the heart and how the environment of Devgarh had contributed to the symptoms. He spoke of the *hridya shanta* herb, of how Ahalya's knowledge had preserved its use as a remedy, and how that wisdom could now be combined with modern medicine.

"The condition you call a curse is real," he said, looking out at the gathered villagers. "It is in your blood, passed down through your families, but it is not something that must control your lives. Ahalya's story was her way of warning you, of helping you to understand this burden. And now, with what I've discovered, we can treat it together—using both the knowledge she left behind and the science that I have studied."

A murmur ran through the crowd, a mixture of disbelief and hope. Ramdas stepped forward, his face a mask of skepticism. "You speak of blending your science with our beliefs, Doctor. But why should we trust you now, after all that has happened?"

Dr. Verma met his gaze, the memory of his own mysterious symptoms still fresh in his mind. "Because I've seen it too, Ramdas. I felt the weight of Ahalya's legacy. I know that it is more than just a story. But I also believe that Ahalya wanted you to find a way to live with this, not to suffer from it. If you give me a chance, I believe we can honor her memory and find peace."

Ramdas studied him for a long moment, the tension in the air palpable. But then, to Dr. Verma's surprise, he gave a slow nod. "Very well, Doctor. You have my blessing to try. But know this—if you fail, it will be the village that pays the price."

Dr. Verma nodded, feeling the weight of responsibility settle back onto his shoulders. But he also felt something else—a glimmer of hope, the sense that perhaps he had finally found a way to bridge the divide between the past and the present.

In the weeks that followed, Dr. Verma began administering the new treatment to a small group of patients, starting with those who had been most severely affected. He carefully monitored their progress, adjusting the dosages as needed and recording their heart rhythms. He explained every step to the patients and their families, making sure they understood the nature of the treatment and the balance he sought between the ancient remedy and modern medication.

To his relief, the results were promising. The patients' heart rhythms began to stabilize, their episodes of chest pain growing less frequent. The villagers, who had once viewed the city doctor with suspicion, began to visit him with gratitude in their eyes, bringing offerings of fruit and freshly baked bread to the clinic.

One evening, as the sun set over the hills of Devgarh, Dr. Verma sat with Ramdas and the village elders by the shrine to Ahalya, their faces softened with the glow of lantern light. They spoke of the past, of the fear that had bound them for so long, and of the future they were just beginning to imagine—a future where the stories of their ancestors could coexist with the knowledge of the present.

Ramdas turned to Dr. Verma, his expression thoughtful. "You have shown us that Ahalya's curse was never about punishment, Doctor. It was about remembering. Perhaps that is why you were meant to come here—to remind us that we are more than just the stories we carry."

Dr. Verma looked out at the darkening forest, where the whispers of the past seemed to mingle with the rustling leaves. He had come to Devgarh as a skeptic, but he was leaving with a deeper understanding of how the heart held onto its secrets—how pain could echo through the generations, and how healing could begin when those echoes were finally heard.

"Thank you, Ramdas," he said quietly. "I think Ahalya would be proud of what we've done together."

And as the night closed in around them, Dr. Verma felt a sense of closure settle over him—a feeling that he had finally uncovered the heart's secret, and in doing so, had found a way to honor both the wisdom of the past and the promise of the future.

Chapter 12: The Last Beat

The monsoon rains swept across the village of Devgarh, drenching the fields and turning the dusty roads into muddy paths. But inside the small clinic that Dr. Arjun Verma had set up, the atmosphere was charged with a different kind of anticipation. It was the day that his first patient, Maya's father, Mr. Kulkarni, was to receive his final check-up before being declared fully recovered.

Maya sat beside her father, her hands folded tightly in her lap. Her eyes, once filled with worry, now shone with hope. Mr. Kulkarni, who had once struggled with every breath, now sat up straight, his face regaining the color that had faded over months of suffering. He gave Dr. Verma a grateful smile as the doctor adjusted the stethoscope over his heart, listening intently.

The familiar rhythm of a steady heartbeat filled Dr. Verma's ears, each beat resonating with the promise of life. He couldn't help but smile as he pulled the stethoscope away, giving Maya a reassuring nod. "Your father's heart is strong. His condition has stabilized, and the symptoms are under control. I believe we can begin to reduce his medication over the next few weeks."

Maya's relief was palpable. Tears welled up in her eyes as she reached for her father's hand, squeezing it gently. "Thank you, Doctor," she whispered, her voice thick with emotion. "I don't know how we could ever repay you."

Dr. Verma shook his head, his expression softening. "There's no need for thanks, Maya. Your father's recovery is thanks enough. This is just the beginning—we still have a long way to go, but it's a start."

Mr. Kulkarni's eyes filled with gratitude as he met Dr. Verma's gaze. "You brought us hope when we had none, Doctor. Ahalya's story was our burden, but you've shown us that it doesn't have to define us."

Dr. Verma nodded, feeling a lump rise in his throat. He had spent so many sleepless nights questioning his decision to follow the path that had led him here, wondering if he was chasing shadows instead of solutions. But now, standing in the warm glow of a family's relief, he knew that the risks had been worth it.

As Maya and her father left the clinic, he watched them disappear into the rain, feeling a quiet sense of fulfillment settle over him. He knew that the recovery of one patient did not guarantee the success of his treatment for everyone, but it was a sign that the path he had chosen was the right one. It was a small victory, but it carried with it the promise of hope for others—hope that they might finally be free of the fear that had shadowed their lives for so long.

The weeks that followed were filled with cautious optimism as more villagers began to respond to the treatment plan. Dr. Verma's blend of the *hridya shanta* herb with modern medication proved effective in stabilizing heart rhythms, allowing those afflicted to regain a sense of normalcy. The villagers, who had once viewed him with suspicion, now greeted him with smiles, offering him their trust and their stories in equal measure.

But even as the days grew brighter, Dr. Verma found himself reflecting on the journey that had brought him here. He spent his evenings walking through the village, watching the children play by the river and the elders gather beneath the banyan tree to share tales of the past. He realized how much his time in Devgarh had changed him—how it had reshaped his understanding of medicine, of healing, and of the thin line between myth and reality.

He had always thought of medicine as a science, a discipline of facts and figures, of diagnoses and treatments. But in Devgarh, he had learned that healing could not be confined to the clinical walls of a hospital. It was something deeper, something that intertwined with the stories people told to make sense of their suffering. Ahalya's curse had been one such story—a way for the villagers to understand the pain that had haunted their families for generations. And by listening to that story, he had found the clues he needed to help them.

He thought of Ahalya often, of the healer who had poured her grief into the land, turning her sorrow into a legacy that spanned centuries. He imagined her standing at the edge of the village, watching over the people she had loved, carrying a burden she could not share. He wondered if, in some way, she had guided him to this place, to the knowledge that had lain buried beneath layers of myth.

One misty morning, Dr. Verma found himself standing at the edge of the village, where the fields gave way to the forest and the path wound up into the hills. He had come here many times during his stay in Devgarh, but today felt different. The air was cool, carrying the scent of damp earth, and the mist curled around the trees like a veil.

He gazed out over the valley, where the rooftops of the village houses shimmered through the fog, their red tiles glinting in the early light. In the distance, he could hear the faint murmur of the river, flowing with the rhythm of life that had persisted in this place long before he had arrived.

As he stood there, a memory surfaced—his first conversation with Ramdas, when the elder had warned him of the dangers of meddling with Ahalya's legacy. He thought of the clash between tradition and science, of the skepticism he had faced from both the villagers and his colleagues. He realized now that the struggle had never been about choosing one over the other; it had been about finding a way to bring them together.

He reached into his pocket and pulled out the brass pendant, turning it over in his hands. Its engravings had faded with time, but he could still trace the outline of the heart that had become a symbol of his journey. He wondered if Ahalya's spirit had finally found peace, knowing that the story she had left behind was being understood in a new way.

Dr. Verma closed his eyes, letting the wind wash over him, and he thought of the lessons he had learned in Devgarh—lessons that had nothing to do with textbooks or clinical trials. He had learned that the heart was more than just an organ; it was a vessel of memory, a keeper of secrets that could span lifetimes. He had learned that healing sometimes required a willingness to listen, to see beyond the surface and into the spaces where science met belief.

And as he stood there, between the forest and the village, he realized that the boundary between myth and reality was not as clear as he had once believed. Perhaps it was not meant to be. Perhaps, like the river that flowed through Devgarh, the two were meant to run together, shaping the landscape in ways that neither could do alone.

With a quiet breath, Dr. Verma turned back toward the village, the pendant still warm in his hand. He knew that his work here was not yet done, that there would be more challenges ahead. But he also knew that he was ready to face them, no longer as a doctor bound by the limits of his training, but as a healer who understood the power of a story.

As the mist lifted and the first rays of sunlight touched the hills, Dr. Verma walked back down the path, his footsteps steady on the earth that held the echoes of the past. And in the distance, the village of Devgarh waited—its heart no longer silent, but beating with the promise of a new beginning.

Thank You for Reading

Dear Reader,

Thank you for embarking on this journey with **The Doctor's Dilemma Collection**. I truly appreciate your time, curiosity, and support in exploring the intricate world of medicine through these stories.

If this book resonated with you or inspired new perspectives, please consider supporting future projects and publications. Your generous contributions make it possible to continue creating meaningful content.

Support My Work:

- **Venmo:** @Nileshlp
- **Cash App:** $drnileshlp
- **BTC**

bc1qs72228z6pauw3rk9tej9f6umu4y9gz289y3cvn

- **ETH**

0xE1DAE6F656c900a4b24257b587ac0856E1e346D2

Every bit of support goes a long way in sustaining my passion for storytelling and public health advocacy.

Once again, thank you from the bottom of my heart. Your encouragement and generosity mean the world to me.

Warm regards,
Dr. Nilesh Panchal
Author and Public Health Practitioner

Don't miss out!

Visit the website below and you can sign up to receive emails whenever Dr. Nilesh Panchal publishes a new book. There's no charge and no obligation.

https://books2read.com/r/B-A-JKGNC-KHIDF

BOOKS 2 READ

Connecting independent readers to independent writers.

Also by Dr. Nilesh Panchal

Clinical Trials Mastery Series
Essentials of Clinical Trials
Clinical Trials: Ethical Considerations and Regulations
Clinical Trials Design and Methodology

Mastering the FDA Approval Process
Mastering New Drug Applications A Step-by-Step Guide
Navigating ANDA: Strategies for Effective Generic Drug Approval
Mastering PMA: A Comprehensive Guide to Premarket Approval for Medical Devices

The Doctor's Dilemma Collection
A Heartbeat Away
Human Trial

Standalone
Navigating FDA Drug Approval
Healthy Habits: A Kid's Guide to Wellness
Mastering Medical Terminology
Navigating the FDA 510(k) Process
Essential First Aid: Life-Saving Techniques for Everyone

Watch for more at https://drmedhealth.com/.

About the Author

Dr. Nilesh Panchal is a distinguished Public Health Practitioner and Health Scientist with over two decades of experience, making significant contributions to the fields of infectious diseases, mental health, and public health education. Holding a DrPH in Public Health Practice, Dr. Panchal is a prolific author known for his ability to translate complex medical concepts into accessible and engaging content for a broad audience. His work, including the acclaimed series "Global Outbreaks: The Saga of Humanity's Health Battles," provides invaluable insights into the challenges posed by infectious diseases, making it an authoritative source for understanding humanity's ongoing battle against deadly pathogens. Dr. Panchal's dedication to educating the public extends to his "Mindfulness and Well-Being Series," where his compassionate and practical approach empowers readers to enhance their mental and emotional well-being.

In addition to his focus on infectious diseases and mental health, Dr. Panchal has made remarkable strides in lifestyle medicine, particularly in the prevention of diabetes. His book series "Healthy Living, Healthy Future: Diabetes Prevention Series" offers evidence-based strategies that empower individuals to make lasting lifestyle changes for a healthier, diabetes-free life. Dr. Panchal's commitment to public health is also reflected in his guide "Essential First Aid: Life-Saving Techniques for Everyone," where he provides clear, step-by-step instructions for managing emergencies. Through his extensive research, Dr. Panchal continues to be a respected voice in global health, contributing to medical journals, speaking at international conferences, and leading health innovation projects aimed at integrating AI into clinical practice. His body of work not only informs but also inspires, making a lasting impact on global health practices and public education.

Read more at https://drmedhealth.com/.

Milton Keynes UK
Ingram Content Group UK Ltd.
UKHW042236011124
450424UK00001BA/19